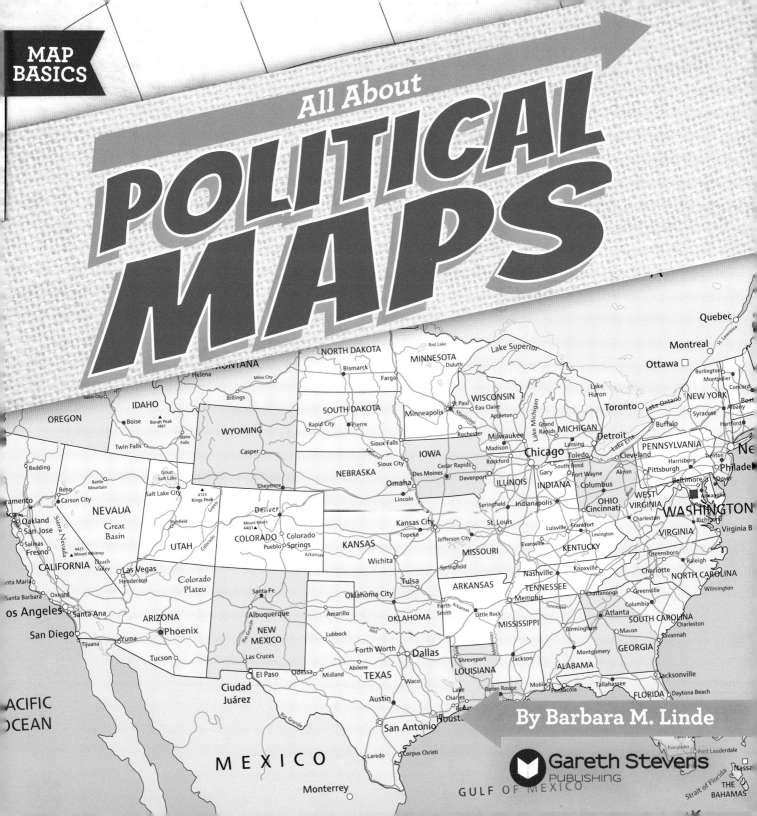

Please visit our website, www.garethstevens.com. For a free color catalog of all our high-quality books, call toll free 1-800-542-2595 or fax 1-877-542-2596.

Cataloging-in-Publication Data

Names: Linde, Barbara M.
Title: All about political maps / Barbara M. Linde.
Description: New York : Gareth Stevens Publishing, 2019. | Series: Map basics | Includes glossary and index.
Identifiers: ISBN 9781538232644 (pbk.) | ISBN 9781538229170 (library bound) | ISBN 9781538232651 (6pack)
Subjects: LCSH: Map reading–Juvenile literature. | Administrative and political divisions–Maps–Juvenile literature.
Classification: LCC GA130.L49 2019 | DDC 912.01'4–dc23

First Edition

Published in 2019 by
Gareth Stevens Publishing
111 East 14th Street, Suite 349
New York, NY 10003

Designer: Sarah Liddell
Editor: Monika Davies

Photo credits: Cover, p. 13 Bardocz Peter/Shutterstock.com; pp. 5, 7, 11, 17, 21 ekler/Shutterstock.com; p. 9 brichuas/Shutterstock.com; pp. 15, 19 Peter Hermes Furian/Shutterstock.com.

Printed in the United States of America

CPSIA compliance information: Batch #CW19GS: For further information contact Gareth Stevens, New York, New York at 1-800-542-2595.

CONTENTS

Words in the glossary appear in **bold** type the first time they are used in the text.

WHAT IS A POLITICAL MAP?

"Political" refers to anything that has to do with government. The government is the system that runs a country, state, city, or town.

A political map is a drawing that shows the governmental **boundaries** of an area. On this political map of the world, white lines indicate, or show, the borders between each country. Each country is shown in a different color. Russia is the largest country in the world. The smallest country is Vatican City, which is inside Italy.

JUST THE FACTS
A person who makes a map is called a cartographer.

POLITICAL WORLD MAP

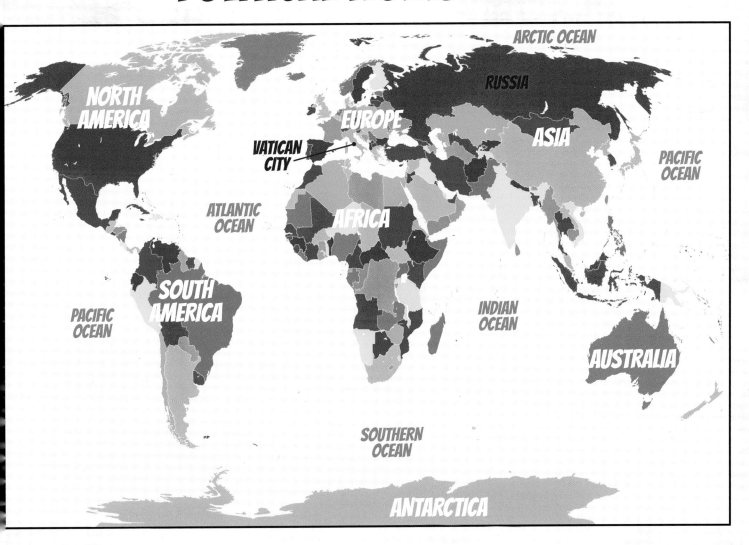

Political maps sometimes use bright colors
so it's easier to tell the countries apart.

NATURAL POLITICAL BORDERS

Natural **landforms**, such as mountains and bodies of water, are sometimes used as political borders. These physical boundaries can protect countries from enemies and keep members of a group together.

Some countries on the **continent** of Europe use natural landforms for all or part of their political borders. For example, the Alps are the mountain range that

separates Italy and France. The Pyrenees are mountains that separate France and Spain. The Danube River forms part of the border between Bulgaria and Romania.

6

POLITICAL MAP OF EUROPE

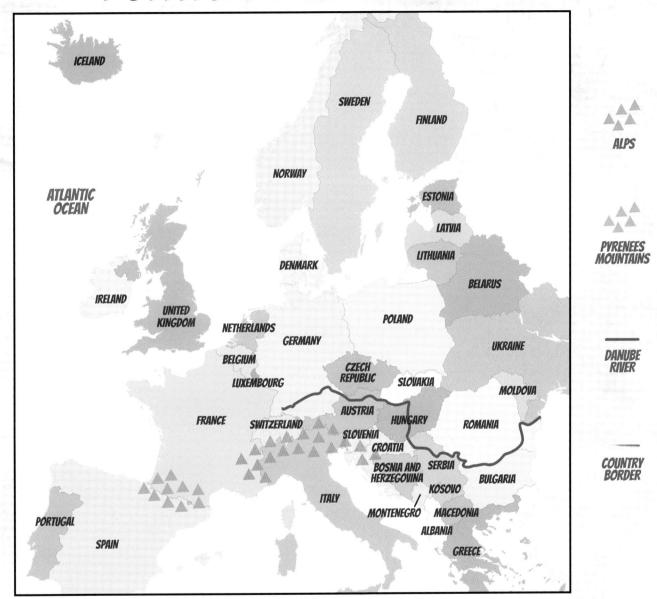

ICELAND

ATLANTIC
OCEAN

SWEDEN

NORWAY

FINLAND

ESTONIA

LATVIA

LITHUANIA

BELARUS

DENMARK

IRELAND

UNITED
KINGDOM

NETHERLANDS

BELGIUM

LUXEMBOURG

GERMANY

POLAND

CZECH
REPUBLIC

SLOVAKIA

UKRAINE

MOLDOVA

FRANCE

SWITZERLAND

AUSTRIA

SLOVENIA

HUNGARY

ROMANIA

CROATIA

BOSNIA AND
HERZEGOVINA

SERBIA

ITALY

MONTENEGRO

KOSOVO

MACEDONIA

BULGARIA

ALBANIA

GREECE

PORTUGAL

SPAIN

ALPS

PYRENEES
MOUNTAINS

DANUBE
RIVER

COUNTRY
BORDER

While natural landforms sometimes shape political
borders, they aren't usually shown on political maps.

7

MAN-MADE POLITICAL BORDERS

Sometimes government leaders meet and choose borders. These political borders are shown with lines on a map. However, these political borders may not be **represented** by a physical boundary, such as a fence. In some places, a small sign might mark a border. You may have seen one of these signs when you entered into a new city or town.

Many states divide their land into smaller sections called counties. Leaders in each county make sure people have electricity, water, and other services.

JUST THE FACTS

In 1876, Texas government leaders said that any new counties in the state should be square as often as possible. They've been that way ever since.

TEXAS COUNTY BORDERS

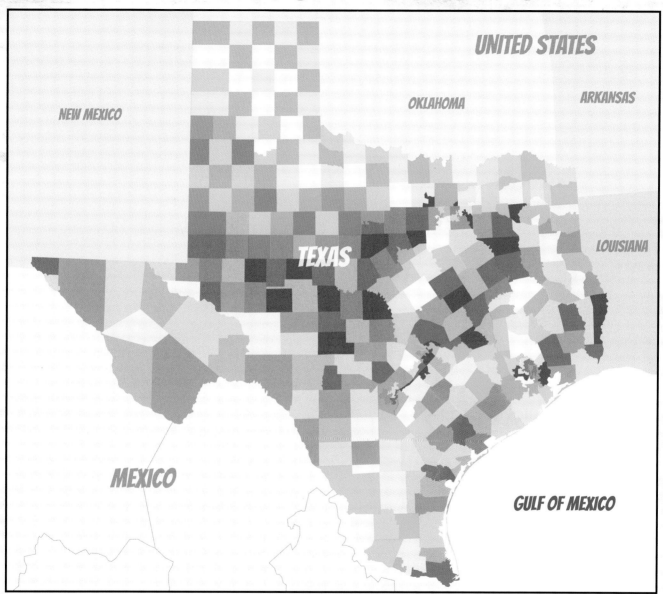

This map of Texas shows the borders for its 254 counties. Texas has more counties than any other state!

USING THE LEGEND

A political map is usually labeled with lines and other **symbols**. The legend is a list that explains what the symbols on a map mean. You can usually find the legend at the bottom of a map. It may be a small box with pictures and text.

The legend on this map of Australia explains that dotted lines represent state boundaries. Each state capital is shown with a white square. The name of the city is next to the square.

JUST THE FACTS

Australia is the world's smallest continent. It's a country made up of six states and 10 **territories**.

POLITICAL MAP OF AUSTRALIA

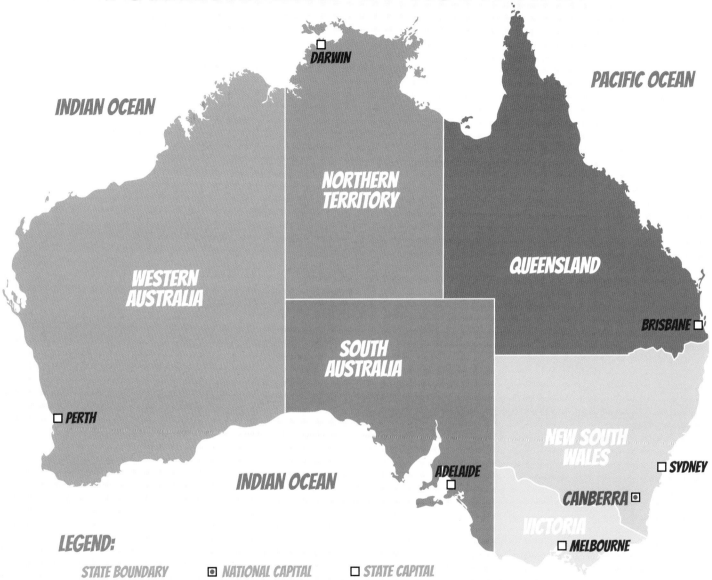

INDIAN OCEAN

PACIFIC OCEAN

DARWIN

NORTHERN TERRITORY

WESTERN AUSTRALIA

QUEENSLAND

BRISBANE

SOUTH AUSTRALIA

PERTH

NEW SOUTH WALES

INDIAN OCEAN

ADELAIDE

SYDNEY

CANBERRA

VICTORIA

MELBOURNE

LEGEND:

STATE BOUNDARY   NATIONAL CAPITAL   STATE CAPITAL

According to this map's legend, the red dot in a white square shows where Canberra, the national capital of Australia, is located.

WHICH WAY?

Which state is south of Maryland and north of North Carolina? A map's **compass rose** will help you find the answer. Look for it at the bottom of the map. The compass rose always shows the cardinal, or main, directions: north, south, east, and west.

This map focuses on the eastern part of the United States. Using the compass rose, you can see that Arkansas is south of Missouri and north of Lousiana. Ohio is west of Pennsylvania, while Alabama is east of Mississippi.

JUST THE FACTS

The top of a map is usually north. This makes the bottom of the map south, the left side west, and the right side east.

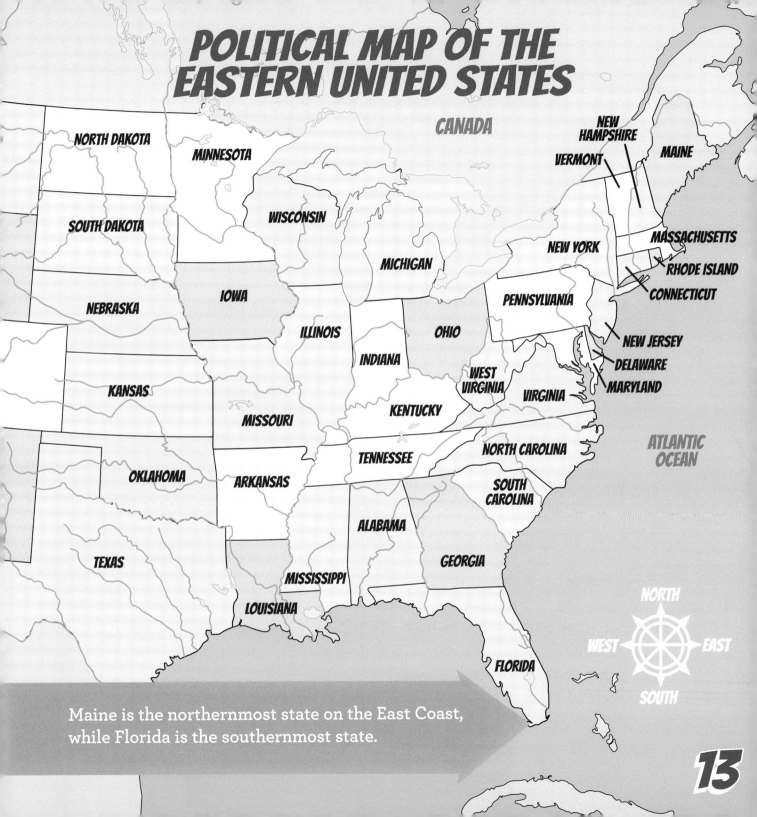

POLITICAL MAP OF THE EASTERN UNITED STATES

CANADA

NEW HAMPSHIRE

VERMONT

MAINE

NORTH DAKOTA

MINNESOTA

WISCONSIN

MICHIGAN

NEW YORK

MASSACHUSETTS

RHODE ISLAND

CONNECTICUT

SOUTH DAKOTA

IOWA

PENNSYLVANIA

NEW JERSEY

DELAWARE

MARYLAND

NEBRASKA

ILLINOIS

INDIANA

OHIO

WEST VIRGINIA

VIRGINIA

KANSAS

MISSOURI

KENTUCKY

NORTH CAROLINA

ATLANTIC OCEAN

TENNESSEE

OKLAHOMA

ARKANSAS

SOUTH CAROLINA

ALABAMA

GEORGIA

TEXAS

MISSISSIPPI

LOUISIANA

NORTH

WEST — EAST

SOUTH

FLORIDA

Maine is the northernmost state on the East Coast, while Florida is the southernmost state.

13

HOW FAR IS IT?

You can find a scale on most maps. A scale looks like a small ruler. Maps show a large area, such as a state, as much smaller than it actually is. A scale uses short **distances** to stand for longer distances.

You can use the scale on a map to figure out the distance between two places. First, measure the distance between two places on the map. Your answer should be in inches. Then, multiply that distance by the number on the scale.

ALASKA

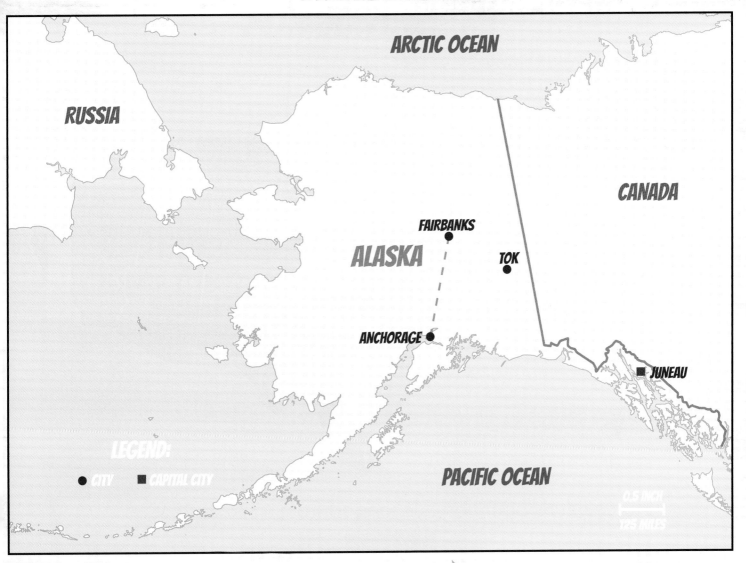

On this map of Alaska, the distance from Anchorage to Fairbanks measures around 1 inch (2.54 cm). According to the scale, 0.5 inch (1.27 cm) equals 125 miles (201 km). This means the distance between the two cities is around 250 miles (402.3 km).

CHANGING OVER TIME

Borders can change because of wars between two countries. The winning country might take over the other country's land, changing the borders of both countries. In the past, borders also changed when one country bought land from another country.

The first map shows the United States in 1776. The second map shows how

the country's boundaries changed from 1776 to 1850. In 1803, the United States made the **Louisiana Purchase** and gained more land. After the Mexican-American War (1846–1848), the United States took over Mexican territory.

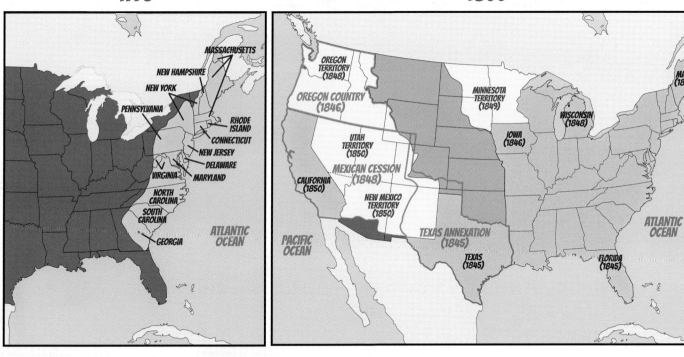

Following the Mexican-American War, the borders of both the United States and Mexico changed.

THE GROWING UNITED STATES

1776

1850

MASSACHUSETTS
NEW HAMPSHIRE
NEW YORK
PENNSYLVANIA
RHODE ISLAND
CONNECTICUT
NEW JERSEY
DELAWARE
VIRGINIA
MARYLAND
NORTH CAROLINA
SOUTH CAROLINA
GEORGIA
ATLANTIC OCEAN

OREGON TERRITORY (1848)
OREGON COUNTRY (1846)
MINNESOTA TERRITORY (1849)
MAINE (1842)
WISCONSIN (1848)
UTAH TERRITORY (1850)
IOWA (1846)
MEXICAN CESSION (1848)
CALIFORNIA (1850)
NEW MEXICO TERRITORY (1850)
PACIFIC OCEAN
TEXAS ANNEXATION (1845)
ATLANTIC OCEAN
TEXAS (1845)
FLORIDA (1845)

LEGEND:

 TERRITORIES

 STATES

FOREIGN AREAS

 UNORGANIZED TERRITORIES

— BORDERS OF EXPANSION

17

CITY MAPS

Another type of political map shows the cities in a state or country. This type of map can help you see how many cities there are in an area and where each city is located.

Political maps of a country often highlight the national capital using a special symbol. A country's national capital is where its government leaders makes decisions. On this map, India's national capital is shown with a red box. State capitals are also often shown on a country map.

MAJOR CITIES IN INDIA

New Delhi is the national capital of India.

MAP IT!

The United States is made up of 50 states. How well do you know your states? Test your knowledge with our quiz!

Use the US political map to answer the questions on the next page. Write your answers on a piece of paper. If you're not sure about a question, ask a classmate for help. Then, compare your answers with the ones listed at the bottom of the page to see how you did. Finally, create your own state questions and quiz your classmates!

KNOW YOUR STATES!

1. WHICH STATE SHARES A BORDER WITH ONLY ONE OTHER STATE?
2. WHICH STATES BORDER MONTANA?
3. WHICH STATE IS BORDERED BY KANSAS TO THE EAST?
4. WHICH STATES ARE WEST OF IDAHO?

4. WASHINGTON, OREGON
3. COLORADO
2. IDAHO, WYOMING, NORTH DAKOTA, SOUTH DAKOTA
1. MAINE

GLOSSARY

boundary: something that marks the limit of an area or place

compass rose: a circular symbol that shows the different directions: north, south, east, and west

continent: one of Earth's seven great landmasses

distance: the amount of space between two places or things

landform: a natural feature of Earth's surface, such as a mountain or valley

Louisiana Purchase: territory of the western United States bought from France in 1803

represent: to stand for

symbol: a picture, shape, or object that stands for something else

territory: an area of land that belongs to or is controlled by a government

FOR MORE INFORMATION

BOOKS

DK Publishing, Inc. *Where on Earth?* New York, NY: DK Publishing, 2017.

National Geographic Society. *National Geographic Student World Atlas.* Washington, DC: National Geographic, 2014.

Phan, Sandy. *Mapping Our World.* Huntington Beach, CA: Teacher Created Materials, 2014.

WEBSITES

Global Trek
teacher.scholastic.com/activities/globaltrek
Take a trip around the world and learn more about the countries you visit along the way.

MapMaker Interactive
mapmaker.nationalgeographic.org
Explore the world using National Geographic's interactive map program.

The US: 50 States - Map Quiz Game
online.seterra.com/en/vgp/3003
Put your US state knowledge to the test with this interactive map quiz!

INDEX